A Lion in Paris

À mon Pata, l'unique à Paris
B. A.

English edition first published 2014 by order of the Tate Trustees
by Tate Publishing, a division of Tate Enterprises Ltd,
Millbank, London SW1P 4RG
www.tate.org.uk/publishing

First published in French as Un Lion à Paris © Autrement 2006
This English edition © Tate 2014
English translation by Rae Walter in association with First Edition Translations Ltd © Tate 2014
Reprinted 2014

Art direction: Kamy Pakdel, studio Autrement
Colour reproduction: Dupont Photogravure
Printed in China by South China Printing Co. Ltd.

A catalogue record for this book is available from the British Library
ISBN 978 1 84976 171 0
Distributed in the United States and Canada by ABRAMS, New York
Library of Congress Control Number applied for

Beatrice Alemagna

A Lion in Paris

TATE PUBLISHING

He was a big lion. A young, curious and lonely lion. He was bored at home on the grasslands,

and so one day he set off to find a job, love and a future.

He arrived in Paris by train, without any luggage. It was the first time he had been in a big city.

Naturally it was a little scary.

The lion waited to see if he would terrify anyone. He wondered if people would start screaming,

if they would step aside in horror as he passed or if they would pursue him with rifle shots.

The people were hurrying around with a strange kind of sword under their arms, but nobody thought about attacking him. That surprised him.

Puzzled, the lion went down into the Metro. The people on the platform hardly even glanced at him.

So then he roared very loudly to make them turn round and look at him.

More than anything, the lion liked to be noticed and he thought it was very sad to be ignored.

When he went out into the street, it started to rain. That made him think of his lovely sunny grasslands

and he felt sad. He turned all grey and shiny like the roofs around him.

In the middle of a square he saw a huge factory, with workers going up and down in a transparent pipe.

The sun came out again, making the building explode into a thousand stars of light. He stood there, gaping at it.

The lion walked along a river, a river that cut the city in half, and the river smiled at him like a mirror.

At last a girl noticed him and her eyes followed him for a while with a loving, tender look.

The lion's heart was beating very fast as he continued his long walk. At the top of an endless flight of steps he saw

a white castle. 'It looks like a cream cake, doesn't it?' said an old lady, smiling at him. 'Grrr,' replied the lion.

They went back down all the steps together.

Then he came to an enormous iron tower and he trembled with fear. He climbed right to the top and the people

down below looked like ants. He absolutely loved it.

The city that had appeared so dreary and frightening and grey in the morning now seemed to be smiling

at him with all its windows.

At a big crossroads, he stopped abruptly. There was a beautiful plinth standing in front of him.

The lion climbed up onto it, put his two paws together and gave a loud roar of joy:

Roaaaaaaar!

Then hundreds of cars tooted their horns to welcome him.

'This is the place for me,' thought the lion, grinning. He looked into the distance and decided to stay.

Perfectly still and happy.

THE END

The lion in this story was inspired by the statue of a lion in the Place Denfert-Rochereau in Paris. It was erected by the architect Frédéric Auguste Bartholdi between 1876 and 1880. I wondered why the Parisians are so fond of this lion. I think it is because he looks very happy where he is.